The McShanes:
Reluctant Warriors

By Conley Stone McAnally

PHARAOH PUBLISHING USA

The McShanes: Reluctant Warriors
By Conley Stone Mcanally

Managing Editor: Richard Andrews
Beta Readers: Kathleen Higgins and Jan Ingram

PHA021 • ISBN 978-0692619957

Pharaoh Publishing USA
www.pharaohpublishingusa.com

Cover art used under license

Produced and designed by Seann McAnally

Also by Conley Stone McAnally

Tales From Homer
Tales From the Lake
Wilson Bay: Tales From an Eskimo Village
Jump, Alaska: Tales From the Interior
O'Brian's Black & Tan: Tales From an Irish Pub
Ashwood: Tales From the Porch
Pantano Wash

Dedicated To:

Pvt. Thomas Conley Copeland,
17th Kansas Infantry Volunteers,
Grand Army of the Republic

Pvt. Joseph Conley McAnally,
3rd Regimental Horse Cavalry

MSG Teddy Stone McAnally,
5th Regiment, 7th Armored Division

Central Missouri State
Fighting Mule Battalion

Past, Present and Future members of the
1/129th Field Artillery Battalion,
Missouri Army National Guard

and

A 'Band of Brothers' too numerous to name

Contents

Hugh McShane   9

Jonas McShane   21

Stephen McShane   26

Scotty McShane   31

Ron McShane   45

Elroy McShane   52

Frank McShane   61

Allen McShane   67

Eloy McShane   77

Baylor McShane   81

Aaron McShane   87

The Last Warrior   98

Chapter 1
Hugh McShane

Hugh McShane was kidnapped by a Spanish raiding party and smugglers as he was tending cattle near his village of Devere, Ireland. He was thrown in the hold of a ship and left there for over a week with nothing to eat and only rancid water to drink. He was eventually traded for a barrel of lemons to Spanish privateers operating between Spain and Hispaniola and along the Spanish Main who were attacking any ship not flying the Spanish flag. They also contracted with the Spanish government to transport gold and silver from Portabella after its trip from the Inca mines in Peru.

The Spanish captain put Hugh to work helping the cook. "Better he is used for something other than rat food in the hold," the chief privateer remarked to the first mate.

While returning to the Caribbean after their second trip back to Spain from Portabella they encountered an English vessel sailing under an English Letter of Marque. A battle ensued with the result being victory for the English.

When the English captain discovered Hugh had been kidnapped and sold to the Spanish for use as a privateer he was aghast until he found out that Hugh was Irish. It was one thing for a fellow Englishman, even a Scotsman, to be kidnapped from his home and made to sail for the Spanish, but such a thing happening to an Irishman made little difference to the captain. He might as well be hanged with the other pirates.

It would not be the first time or the last time the luck of the Irish served the McShane family. During the battle the English cook had lost his right arm. The captain ordered Hugh to be the cook's assistance and to do all the work needed to be done that could not be done by a one-armed cook. When Hugh suggested that he be allowed to go home because he was not interested in a life at sea, the captain was outraged by the arrogance and struck Hugh repeatedly about the head.

Hugh spent the next several months serving King and Country helping the cook feed those fighting the Spanish, the French, and any other country not flying an English flag. Unlike the Spanish, when a ship was to be attacked, the cook, which meant Hugh now because of the cook's absent arm, was expected to partake in the battle.

At first it was difficult to harm let alone kill someone, like himself, who was probably only fighting because he was told to and afraid of what would happen to him if he didn't. Eventually he got to the point where he felt no remorse after a battle and would go below deck and help the cook prepare the victory meal.

Hugh realized that no matter how hard he tried, nor how hard he worked, it was never good enough. The one-armed cook constantly berated him, the captain and first mate would constantly cuff him up the side of the head, and all but one of the crew made it be known that no Irishman was their equal.

The only member of the crew who had befriended him was a dark skin free black named Kona from Portabella. He said his mother was a Queen from Africa. She had been betrayed by the people in her village and sold to Arabs then to the Portuguese and eventually to a plantation owner near Portabella. Kona's father was the plantation owner.

The plantation grew bananas and coconuts along with fresh fruit and sold them to the caravans bringing gold and silver across the isthmus from Peru. Kona's father decided to develop another plantation on the Pacific side of the isthmus so he could sell supplies to those crossing over to the Atlantic.

Kona, along with his father and several slaves, headed towards the Spanish fort that protected Spanish interests on the Pacific side of the New World. After two days Kona's father fell sick with a fever and was not able to continue. The slaves took advantage of the situation and took what supplies there were and ran off to the interior where they hoped to join others who had done the same from time to time. Kona remained behind.

Kona bathed and wiped his father's brow. He burned leaves from a nearby plant that his Queen mother had told him had medicinal powers. She said they had similar plants back in her village in Africa. She had taught Kona which plants and berries could be eaten and which could not. She taught him as much as she knew about the jungle and the spirits that dwell there. She was not a witch as the village shamans had claimed but she did possess a power to understand people and events that surrounded her and the ability to say and do the right thing at the right time. To augment her mental capacity she was a strong and stately woman standing well over six feet.

On one of their many walks of exploring what mysteries the surrounding jungle kept hidden, Queen and Kona stopped on a black sand beach to rest and gazed past the lagoon well out into the Atlantic. Kona asked her if she missed her home in Africa. She said she missed her home as it was at one time but not what it turned into. "My own people are the ones that sold me to the Arabs. I was their Queen, but the jealous ones, those who did not have my gift, convinced the people I was a witch because of the things that I predicted always came to pass. They gained the confidence of the people and, well here I am. But all is well; my owner, your father, is kind and I can be Queen of all we see, and you my son will one day be the king and your children will be either kings or queens forever."

As Kona wiped the face of his father and practiced

the art of healing like the Queen had shown him
his father's fever dissipated. Kona brewed some
tea from some roots and provided fruit and as his
father's health improved, introduced fish and nuts
to the diet. Gradually his father gained strength
enough to walk with the help of Kona back to
Portabella and his plantation.

A few years passed and Kona's father felt
it necessary to return to Spain to inspect his
warehouses - he decided to take Kona with him.

A week out of port their ship was attacked by an
English vessel and all aboard were taken prisoner
and hanged save Kona. Kona's father from the
gallows stated that Kona was a free black and not a
slave regardless of the lack of documentation.

The only redeeming quality held by the English
captain was that he was an abolitionist. He gave
Kona a legal writ declaring his manumission. The
captain was also short handed and pressed Kona
into service. When Hugh pointed out the absurdity
of the situation, Kona just shrugged his shoulders
and said, "With freedom comes a price. I will go
back to my kingdom some day."

During the night watch many miles north of
the Spanish Main, Hugh decided that he had one
too many incidents with the cook, a smart mouth
midshipman, the first mate and the captain. It was
the unfortunate luck of the midshipman that he
had cuffed Hugh up the side of the head on that
particular night and there was no one else awake on
board. Hugh had had enough. Hugh cracked the

young officer over the head with a cast iron pot and tossed the body over the side of the ship. Hugh had no plan as what to do next but he noticed land off the starboard. He jumped overboard and swam to shore.

He walked out of the ocean, walked across a rock beach and into a thick forest. He had no idea where he was. The midshipman and he would not be missed till the morning, several hours hence, but he headed inland as fast as his feet would take him nonetheless. He didn't think anyone saw him throw the body overboard or jump into the sea but he wasn't going to take any chances. He reasoned the captain would waste little time looking for him though. A reluctant Irish sailor, a troublesome one at that, was not that important to back track and search for.

The thick forest he found himself in widened out a little after a mile or two inland. At least he could see the sky and the sun coming up over his shoulder through the thicket. He did not stop walking west until the sun was overhead. As he sat down he was lucky to have picked a cherry tree to rest under. He ate his fill and then drifted off into an exhausted dreamless sleep.

He must have slept the entire day and night because the sun was coming up in about the same place he remembered it coming up previously. He had a raging thirst and knew he had to find water and something more substantial to eat than cherries. If only he had planned better or for that fact, he thought to himself, "If I had only planned at all."

His father had always told him that the Irish were lucky and Papa was proven right. Hugh came across a little creek less than a mile from the cherry tree and he followed it up stream, knowing that to go down stream would take him closer to the ocean.

Again the luck of the Irish was with him. He came to a wide deep spot in the creek featuring turtles galore. As he caught one turtle he noticed some fish close by. He thought to himself that he could do quite well living on turtle, fish, and cherries.

He smashed the turtle open with a rock and was about to eat it raw when he thought turtle meat would probably taste better cooked. He was in no hurry at the present. He built a fire using a method the ships cook used when flint was not available. Two sticks, twine and kindling was all that was needed. He could not remember eating a more delectable meal.

Later that day he fashioned a wooden spike and tried his luck spearing a couple of fish. He was successful enough that he ate well again that evening and the next morning.

Hugh's dark skinned friend, Kona had described building huts from sticks, grass, and palms. Hugh directed his energy to doing just that. He knew he would need some kind of protection from the elements eventually. The weather had been agreeable but he could not count on it always being that way.

After a day constructing the dwelling he stood

back and took a good look. He had used sticks intertwined and secured them with strips of bark. He laid thick thatch over the top and around the side he stacked sod and doubled the amount along the base and configured it to slow seepage during the wet season and with sloped edges to drain water coming from the ruff away from the base. In addition he packed mud on the exterior wall and then on the inside where he noticed light penetrating. Hugh planned on staying there a long time. He had everything he needed and had not been as comfortable or content for a very long time. He remembered how he would snare fox and hares back in Ireland and thought he would give that a go. Surely there were animals like that about.

After a month Hugh woke one morning to the smell of meat cooking and voices coming just outside his abode. He froze and felt on the verge of panic. His first thought was that the English captain had decided to hunt him down or there was a press gang waiting to haul him off to a waiting ship. He grabbed a log he had fashioned into club in one hand and his fishing spear in the other, vowing never to return to the life of a seaman.

He sprang from the shelter only to see three very large men sitting around a camp fire. The three men were startled at first but then looked at each other and then back at Hugh then back towards each other again and started laughing.

"You will be laughing out the other side of your face," said Hugh

"Settle down me lad. We're not here to laugh at you. But do ya have any idea how ridiculous you look with a stick in one hand and a silly looking spear in another, naked and hairy faced. Sit me friend and have some turkey."

Hugh was confused and a little embarrassed by his appearance so he quickly put on his only pair of pants that covered just a little bit more than when he was naked and sat down as the stranger had requested. The stranger handed him what looked like a giant chicken leg. Hugh did not know what a turkey was but he enjoyed it nonetheless.

The stranger was an inn operator at a place called Lydia's Landing. His two companions were his cousins named Ronny and Stephen. "We are from the McJonas clan up in the hills. Amos is my name. We have been trying to track down a couple of thieves who broke into our settlement and stole most of the food from our larder. Winter 'tis a coming sooner than ya think and our little community needs all the food that we stored - and more.

"Sorry we startled you but when we came upon your place here we first thought it might have been the thieves, but when we saw you had no horses anywhere we realized our mistake. Thought we would use your fire pit here nonetheless, didn't think you'd mind, besides that you were fast asleep."

"For that other leg of what you call a turkey I'll let you all stay as long as you'd like," said Hugh through a mouth full of the fowl.

The next morning Amos, Ronny and Stephen were preparing to continue their search for the larder thieves. Amos suggested Hugh join them, "You would be more than welcome. You have a nice place here but these woods can be dangerous to one man living alone. Besides I don't see you have your own larder. You will need it for the coming winter. It is bound to be a hard one. We will share what we retrieve from the thieves and between the four of us restock our house and yours."

Hugh thought the situation over and said he would accompany them but he didn't have clothes or a weapon of any kind. Amos told him that could be taken care of and produced a pair of pants and a brown leather shirt along with a flintlock pistol. "We will get you a coat later when we find the larder thieves. We can't give you a horse as you might have guessed so you'll have to walk. The tracking will go slow for the most part so you won't have any trouble keeping up. If we move a little fast from time to time we can always double up for a while."

After only a day of tracking the four came across the remains of what looked like the thieving bunch. The remains of three men lay before them, all hacked to death and mutilated. Hugh had seen many a dead man, even killed more than most for one his age, but even the cat-a-nine tails and keel-hauling could not compare to the brutality he gazed upon.

Hugh's three companions seemed indifferent to the fate of the thieves and more concerned about gathering up the bags that the attackers had left. Amos said that the dried meat was gone and the only things left were sacks and barrels of dried fruit, vegetables, and an ample supply of seed corn.

"Must have been some renegade Indians," Amos said. "They only took what they could eat on the trail. It is not a tribe from around here that did such a thing. All of them have lived in the same spot for years. Got their own fields and would have taken the seed corn." Turning to Hugh, "I thought you were Irish due to that lilt, you were lucky those renegades didn't find you instead of them thieves."

Hugh wanted to return to his little place after he had helped find what remained of the larder but he knew Amos had a point. He took Amos up on his offer to return to Lydia's Landing and join them in hunting to replenish their meat supply.

Hugh's hunting to fill the larder with meat and his work around the landing earned him the respect of the McJonas clan. So much so that Amos suggested he give up his place and move in with them at least for the winter. "If it don't work out, your place ain't a goin nowhere, it will be there next spring."

He thought about it for awhile and then told Amos yes, he would stay at least thru the winter. The luck of the Irish had descended on him again, it turned out to be the coldest and bitterest winter anyone in the area could remember.

As he lay next to the hearth night after night it reminded him of a life he had almost forgotten. He grew to miss his home in Ireland more and more.

He had disciplined himself not to think about his town of Devere and his family and all that he once held dear. He felt at peace and not fearful of the future. There was hope. The past was just that - the past.

He began to think that he would like to start a family of his own and that Amos's daughter Charlotte might be the place to start. It was a distinct possibility. He noticed her sideway glances more than once. She might be interested. God knew that there were not that many men with out the last name of McJonas lurking about. He would talk to Amos on the morrow.

Chapter 2
Jonas McShane

Jonas had heard his grandfather tell about fighting the Spanish and the French while he was a sailor in the English Navy. When he was young this always confused Jonas a little because Grandfather said he hated the English. "Why," the young Jonas asked himself, "would anyone fight for someone that they hated?" He almost found out how such a thing could happen by narrowly escaping a press gang while visiting his cousin in Boston.

He had delivered a load of seed corn to a mill near Boston and since he had never been to the city he decided to pay a visit to his cousin he had not seen for a year or so. He found Ronny McDougal who was the great-grandson of Ronny McJonas, the cousin of Amos, Jonas's great-grandfather.

Ronny and Jonas picked up where they had left off, like a year had not passed since their last visit. Jonas stayed a few more days in Boston than he intended. Ronny had introduced him to some friends and they all spent a lot of time discussing things like taxes and representative democracy. The ideas he heard from the group were new to Jonas and he did not understand the concepts and knew little about any of the topics discussed. Jonas did not have to understand the topics however to realize that the men were angry men. Men who thought injustices were being done and were searching for a common ground to rectify the wrongs as they appeared to them.

One of the younger men, who had been stationed at the pub door one evening when the group was meeting, came bursting into the room and told them that the British press gangs were on the prowl and getting dangerously close. Ronny and his band immediately went out the back door and Jonas quickly followed. Jonas was separated from the group because he stumbled in the alley behind the inn and luckily fell behind a water barrel where he was hidden as the press gains ran past. He regained his footing and no one was around. He scampered to the top of the inn using a drain pipe and watched as the press gang took two into custody the next street away. They had not left the inn fast enough. That seemed to satisfy the pursuers and they left the area with their two new recruits in tow.

Jonas made his way back to the McDougal house and bid them a farewell. He was going back to the safety of Lydia's Landing.

When he returned, Jonas reported to his father what had transpired in Boston and the discussions he had with Ronny and his friends. Samuel, Jonas's father, said that it sounded like a revolution would soon be upon them unless people like Ronny and his friends realized that the British Empire was to large for a bunch of farmers and shop keepers to take on.

Samuel had no great love for the English - he remembered stories his father Hugh had told him – but he did not have the same hatred as his father. Jonas was indifferent to the English altogether. Hugh was gone now and Samuel and Jonas were reluctant to risk the life they had built on abstract principals they did not comprehend. They did not feel threatened, they had no personal animosity towards the Redcoats - the ones who would actually do the fighting and dying if war came - none of their current relatives were harmed by King George, nor were any of their neighbors. Nothing was personal and Samuel didn't want it to become so. If things did get personal, than that was a different story. That is why when Jonas received a letter from Ronny asking that he attend a meeting in a little town called Lexington close to Boston, Samuel urged Jonas to go. "Perhaps you can talk some sense into that boy. Bring the lad back here. Back to Lydia's Landing where his roots are. Convince him to let this folly go." Jonas was reluctant to go but did as his father wished. He wanted to stay as far away from Boston as he could and the tone of Ronny's letter concerned him.

The meeting was everything Jonas feared. The men of Lexington and neighboring Concord were hiding guns and ammunition around town, on farms and in the woods. The British officials in Boston viewed such an act as dangerous to the Crown. The men of Lexington and Concord heard that a contingent of British soldiers was planning on confiscating their munitions. This could not be tolerated the men of the village vowed.

Ronny would not listen to Jonas's pleading to return with him to Lydia's Landing. He was talking to Ronny when a rider came galloping by and yelled out that the British would be there in the morning. Ronny grabbed a musket and prepared for what was to come the following day.

Jonas was still trying to talk sense into Ronny - at least from Jonas's standpoint - as the men lined up on the Commons. The British appeared in the distance marching towards the village with their drums beating and flags waving. Within a few yards the Redcoats formed a battle formation but kept their guns at port arms. The British were a formidable sight Jonas thought.

There was quiet. Neither side budged. No one was pointing a weapon. Jonas hoped one side or the other would return to from where they came. There was fear in the eyes of the men who had gathered on the commons that day on both sides. No one wanted a fight but each had what they deemed their duty. The time dragged on then stood still. There was a shot, then another, then more shots, then confusion on the side of the British. The British started backing away.

Ronny was shot and killed soon after the firing

commenced. Instinctively, Jonas picked up the musket of his fallen cousin and returned fire, and returned fire again. Things became personal after that. Jonas helped the rag-tag militia chase the British back to Boston.

Jonas McShane ended up serving in the Continental Army for the next several years fighting the Redcoats from New York to Philadelphia. He rose in rank and eventually became a member of General Lafayette's staff and was present at Yorktown to watch Cornwallis's surrender.

CHAPTER 3
Stephen McShane

The War of 1812 and the Mexican War did
not find a McShane in attendance. After the
Revolutionary War, Jonas and many like him
were given tracts of land west of the Alleghany
Mountains. There he raised a family. His oldest
boy Hugh moved to an area that is now St. Louis,
Missouri and started a tanning company where he
took advantage of the beaver trade. Hugh's two sons
eventually ventured into the buffalo hide curing
business and did not find it necessary to engage
in any wars that seemed to be just on the fringe of
destroying their way of life. However, when the
civil war came along things were a little different.

Abernathy and Stephen McShane were making a
lot of money on trading buffalo hides in St. Louis
for beef cattle and selling the cured meat to the
Army. Fort Sumter came along, however, and
Stephen got appointed by the Missouri Governor
to the Federal Quartermaster Corps as a captain
in charge of procurement of foodstuffs for the
Missouri Sector. Stephen was reluctant to take the

appointment but Abernathy convinced him that it would be good for their business. "The Army has to buy their meat somewhere from someone; it might as well be us." Stephen thought the whole thing must be illegal so when he did purchase from his brother he always made sure that he paid him less than he would have anyone else. Prices were so inflated for foodstuffs that there was still a bunch of money to be made. Abernathy thought it was a good idea to handle things that way, like he always said, "pigs get fat and hogs get butchered."

Stephen was making such an impression on the War Department in his financial transactions and the way he saved the military money, much more than others holding the same position in other portions of the country, that they sent him to Washington D.C. to work in the central procurement department.

He was doing fine, mostly by getting lost in the large bureaucracy, until he started dating the daughter of his supervisor who just happened to be a Brigadier General. The Brigadier did not approve and to break the steamy romance up the Brigadier transferred Stephen to an infantry regiment. He was to be the Regimental Equipment Procurement Officer.

Stephen had no idea how to go about his job but it didn't matter because as soon as he arrived at his new duty station the regiment was attacked by a Confederate brigade. His first thought was how to get away from the fighting but before he could make up his mind he was jumped on by a scrawny confederate soldier who Stephen figured out real quick was trying to do him bodily harm. He had no choice but defend himself and somehow managed to throw the young man to the ground and pierce his side with a bayonet. As Stephen stood there watching the life drain out of the rebel he was shot in the leg just below the knee. While trying to regain his feet by using his rifle for a crutch he fell backwards and his weapon discharged striking another confederate soldier in the chest who was about to bayonet the Regimental Colonel. The percussion of the rifle knocked Stephen to the ground and he landed on a bayonet piercing his shoulder.

The Union held the day and the battlefield at Spotsylvania started swarming with medics and ambulances.

Stephen recovered from his wounds and transferred to Company A of the 69th Volunteer Infantry Regiment as its captain as a reward for his bravery in saving the Regimental Colonel's life. A battalion commander in the 69th had witnessed Stephen's performance in battle and mistook acrobatic mishaps for bravery and skill in warfare.

Later that year Stephen was trying to break up a fight between two of his noncommissioned officers when a pistol accidentally discharged and the bullet lodged just below his knee close to his other wound. This just so happened to take place right before a confederate raiding party galloped over the ridge at a place call Manson Hill, Virginia. It was assumed by his superiors that he had received his wound in battle – the two sergeants being killed in the attack and thus no one to dispute the assumption – and Stephen was again honored for bravery and he hoped he would finally be sent home. He was really reluctant to go anywhere else.

Stephen was not spared yet. He was made a Major in the regiment and for a reward received a head wound at Gettysburg defending the bloody angle and at Cold Harbor he got shot in the leg again after the explosion and infamous attack. The surgeon decided that they would amputate his leg this time but some how Stephen talked him out of it. His fighting days were done however. He was discharged and sent back to St. Louis and worked with his brother in the tanning business.

The Brigadier who had tried to break up the romance between Stephen and his daughter was so impressed with Stephen's war record he consented when Stephen asked him for his daughter's hand in marriage.

He never tired telling his children and grandchildren about his war experience and heroic exploits while serving in the Grand Army of the Republic. The stories became more heroic as the years passed by. He felt his serving in the Army was the most significant thing he had ever done in his life.

He compiled his memoirs and wrote a short history of the 69th Volunteer Infantry Regiment.

He became an active member in the Civil War Union Veteran's Association and he never missed a regimental reunion.

CHAPTER 4
Scotty McShane

Scotty McShane, grandson of Stephen, was getting rather bored working as a procurement clerk in the family business. He craved adventure but not enough to do anything that might put him in harm's way. Scotty was a little reluctant to join the Army due to the accounts he had heard Grandpa McShane tell about his experiences in the Civil War. But when he heard through a business contact that the United States Army needed procurement officers for a canal that President Roosevelt was undertaking, it piqued his interest. In checking further he got somewhat distressed to find that to be a procurement officer for the Panama Canal project one really needed to be an officer with a big 'O' which meant joining the Army. However, although President Roosevelt wanted to be a big player on the world stage, Scotty knew the country was not ready for another war anytime soon.

He read all the books that were available in the St. Louis County Library that had anything to do with Panama, Columbia, the Isthmus of Panama, climatic conditions and specifically how not to contract malaria, typhoid or yellow fever, and cholera. He pretty well made up his mind that he would be just as safe in a nice office in Panama City handing out contracts as he would be sitting in a stuffy office along the Mississippi River with the occasional business trip to New Orleans. He only saw one inconvenience in his plan and that is when he approached Grandpa Stephen.

Scotty's grandfather was delighted that Scotty was going to join the Army and help build what some had already predicted would be one of the great engineering feats of the 20th century. Scotty told Grandpa Stephen about his concern and the former civil war hero understood immediately. He contacted one of his regimental brothers who he knew had a son working in the war department and was able to get Scotty a direct commission as captain in the quartermaster corps. He didn't even need to go to basic training. Scotty was relieved. His only concern was no more.

With a brand new uniform and military style briefcase, Scotty boarded a train to New York City, then a steamship where he immediately got seasick and stayed seasick until the USS Grant rounded the tip of Florida. One week later, after the Grant anchored just off the coast of Panama near a small village called Portabella, he and several other soldiers joined a pack-mule train and headed overland to Panama City. It was not a pleasant trip but it was considered adventurous if sleeping in the mud, riding poled rafts over lakes and small rivers and swatting flies and mosquitoes big enough to have wood ticks attached, or so the men said with typical military gallows humor.

The convoy, if one could so call such a dismal looking affair, arrived at the outskirts of Panama City at Fort Griffin. Scotty immediately reported to the Group Commander of the 3rd Panama Construction Division, Major General Henry. Major General Henry knew of Scotty's political connections. Being a Major General he wanted to be a Lieutenant General before he was forced to retire so he gave Scotty what the general thought would be a pretty plush assignment. With orders firmly in hand Scotty headed back across the trail he just came this time headed for Fort Sheridan as the chief procurement officer of the 45th Brigade.

The commander of the 45th Brigade was Brigadier Patrick Cavanaugh, a West Point classmate of Henry's. Neither man liked the other very much, but both were usually able to put their personal problems aside when it came to professional military matters.

General Cavanaugh's first impression of Captain McShane was good but he resented what he felt was Henry's interference in how Cavanaugh ran his brigade. Instead of Chief Procurement Officer for the brigade, Cavanaugh assigned Scotty to a brand new "but very important position," as he told Captain McShane. Cavanaugh explained to Scotty that as Chief Procurement Officer of Environmental

Friendly Food Items, "Your responsibility will be to ensure that all foodstuffs purchased, requisitioned, or confiscated from or by indigenous forces in or around the Panama Canal Zone be of the purest and highest quality possibly obtainable and at a competitive price within standards as prescribed by the War Department. Do not make any direct purchase, however, until you receive specific guideline specifications from me. I cannot emphasize it enough . . . do nothing until you hear from me. Our relationship with the people of Panama can be prickly; we don't want to slight them unintentionally." In other words, Scotty rightfully concluded, 'find yourself a place to set up operations but don't do anything unless you hear from me, and you probably won't. Don't piss anyone off and we will get along just fine.' Captain Scotty McShane thought that was a splendid idea.

General Cavanaugh did not put any restraints or give any guidance on where Scotty could set up operations or if he was to have a staff. Not realizing the protocol in requisitioning supplies and personnel Scotty marched into the personnel office and demanded he immediately be assigned a personal aide, interpreter, and clerk. He left the office with a first aid kit, a typewriter, and an English to Spanish dictionary. He then went to the transportation department where he said his position and rank entitled him to two horses and three pack mules. He left the department with one broken down mule, but at the last minute was supplied a map of the Atlantic coastline by a private who had more smirk than smile.

Scotty next went to the base supply division and was more successful after handing over three tins of Prince Albert and enough paper to roll many a smoke. He managed to pack thirty days of supplies on his assigned mule, another mule he found wandering around between the transportation department and supply division, and a horse that was tied up outside of the medical tent. He figured the owner was probably sick or injured and would not need his horse for awhile.

After securing all the necessary items on the back of the beasts, he hastily beat a quick retreat out of the cantonment area, making sure not to go back past the hospital tent. He would consult his map just as soon as there was a little distance between him and anyone that might be looking for a stray horse and mule.

About five miles out of Fort Sheridan, Scotty stopped to get his bearings. The map he had been provided was adequate for following the coastline and within five to ten miles inland, but for more than that it was pretty useless. He decided he would make camp for the night and head for the coast the next morning and start south or at least to his right. Panama was one of the few places where you could watch the sun rise in the Pacific Ocean and set in the Atlantic, or so it seemed. The phenomenon had no effect on Scotty, he knew where north was and he could always find the ocean.

He started a fire, drank water heavily, and hung a hammock so as not to mingle with the creepy crawly things he had read about during his research at the St. Louis Library. His readings at the library did not prepare him for the strange sounds from the jungle night. Animal sounds didn't bother him but the movement of leaves, trees, and bushes just out of sight from the light of the fire kept him awake. Also, he felt the eerie sensation he was being watched or studied. He finally drifted off to a restless sleep - the kind of sleep that you don't know has happened until you look at the horizon and see that there is a glow. He broke camp quickly and moved rapidly to the south, or at least in the direction where the Atlantic and its beaches were always on his left.

The next night he bivouacked on the beach after ensuring he was above the high tide mark. Things were much more serene and peaceful that night but he still could not shake the feeling that he was being watched as he sat around the camp fire studying his map. He knew that he would have to establish some sort of base camp soon and inform General Cavanaugh of his location. The last thing he wanted was to be deemed a deserter. He came to no conclusion that night. While making coffee the next morning a soldier on horseback came from the direction Scotty was going. The rider stopped and dismounted, saluted and asked in a respectful way if "the Captain would mind sharing some of the coffee brewing." "Certainly I would not mind," was the

Captain's reply.

The horseman was a dispatch rider for the 45th Engineering Brigade. He informed Scotty that he rode the same course every two weeks delivering orders, military dispatches, and personal mail to those along his route. Scotty had the trooper point out places on the map that might be good to set up his office and begin reconnaissance of foodstuffs just in case General Cavanaugh did contact him. With the carrier's help Scotty settled on a spot along a small lagoon called Nombre de Dios. 'Name of God' or something like that his Spanish translation book informed him. The God part was what interested him the most. He wasn't much of a church going type of guy but he could tell that if he did much exploring or adventure seeking he might need all the help he could get and why not at least stack the odds in his favor by living with a name of God. Perhaps it was God that was watching him during the night, he thought, but not all that seriously.

Scotty thought it only prudent that he send an official correspondence to the General and let him know where he was just in case anyone ever asked. Scotty quickly jotted down his approximate intended whereabouts and told the rider to give the message directly to General Cavanaugh. "From your hand to his," Scotty ordered realizing that was the first order he had given that he felt might be obeyed without a Prince Albert can in the mix.

The messenger and Scotty shared one more pot of

coffee, and half way through, Scotty mentioned the strange feeling he had about being watched during the evening and while he slept. The rider told him that was something that occurred a lot in the jungle and especially in this part of Panama. "They say it is the Conga Queen looking for a mate that is worthy of her. She watches and makes a decision then weaves a spell that no man can escape. It is nothing to be concerned about. There really is a Conga Queen, though. She goes from village to village celebrating some sort of African tradition from time to time. Doesn't ever seem to be a set schedule of when or where she appears until about a day ahead. I have never been able to determine just what it is that she is supposed to be celebrating but she does no one harm or evil. Nor does the legend ever say that she does anything good either come to think of it. Don't concern yourself, really."

Two weeks after sending his official dispatch and after settling in to his requisitioned office and quarters he received a reply by the twice a month military carrier. It read "From Cavanaugh: Good."

Scotty had no authority to requisition anything but after befriending the self- appointed mayor or chief of Nombre - he never could tell what the man's official title was - he was introduced to a large black lady who he was to call Mama Niambi. She had a large thatched hut, bigger than most in the village, Scotty noticed, and thought it was so designed to match her size and most importantly she was more than willing to share half her abode next to the lagoon with him at a very reasonable price. One side of the hut would be his office and sleeping quarters and the other side would be her living area and between them was a room that resembled a kitchen. She charged him one dollar a month.

During the negotiation phase when he pretended to balk at the price she countered that for another dollar a month she would cook for him. Such a deal he could not pass up.

It did not take Scotty two weeks to scout out the surrounding area and make verbal agreements with the few coconut and banana growers in the region to provide the Army with their entire crop if and when the Army felt it necessary. The growers didn't mind the loose arrangement and agreement because they never sold their crops to anyone anyway, they just used it for the feeding of their families and trade material for fish that they didn't catch themselves from the lagoon. Technically, given his instructions from General Cavanaugh, he should not have made contact with any of the growers but "better to be ready just in case and the general is a long ways away." Scotty surmised.

With all the free time on his hands, Scotty began riding deeper and deeper into the jungle but always with a guide. He kept good records of all he saw and drew pretty good likenesses of the flora and fauna he observed. He always returned before sundown each night. The dark of the jungle still haunted him and he noticed his guide was eager to get back to Nombre before the sun went down too.

One evening while sitting with Mama Niambi on the front porch, he mentioned the legend he heard about the Conga Queen. Mama Niambi just laughed and said yes, that she had heard the legend ever since she was a little girl and that the Conga Queen must be getting pretty old and desperate by now so he better watch out. She just might choose him as being worthy. "There will be a celebration soon by the representative of the Conga Queen. No one knows when exactly but it will happen. Sort of like your Christian Christmas but without a fixed date. There will be prizes and a dance, a real overall celebration. I am just teasing about being chosen by the Conga Queen. You are much too skinny and pale to be of any interest to her." With that Mama Niambi put her hand over her mouth and tried to stifle a laugh.

Three months went by and no one mentioned the Conga Queen or when the festival might begin and there had been no word from anyone in the Army except the bimonthly dispatch rider and the every-two-week supply wagon. Both the dispatch rider and the supply wagonmaster, it became clear, only stayed all night in Nombre because that is where each had a female companion – but, unfortunately, the same one.

Scotty could see a problem brewing and did a quick calculation and found that the two would not be in the village at the same time for over four months. He wasn't real sure that both men didn't know about the other anyway because everyone in the village knew. Now that Scotty became aware of the situation he thought that perhaps he should inform someone up the chain of command but then decided not to interfere. Perhaps he would be gone in four months and it would be someone else's problem.

One evening after watching Mama Niambi prepare a freshly caught octopus for dinner, Scotty heard a melodic sound coming from across the lagoon. It was a soprano sort of sing-song chant with a syncopated beat of several drums. He asked Mama Niambi what it was. She nonchalantly said it was the village maidens practicing for the arrival of the Conga Queen the next night and she continued preparing the octopus. After several attempts at soliciting more information as to what was to happen and failing, Scotty decided he would just have to wait.

No one mentioned the Conga Queen or the upcoming festival all the next day. Mama Niambi went ahead and prepared dinner as usual. After they had eaten, Scotty could not stand it any longer and demanded that he be given some sort of explanation as what to expect. After he finished his childish tirade, a man appeared at the kitchen door and requested that Scotty accompany him. "The Conga Queen says the festivities will not commence until the white soldier appears. You will come with me Captain," the stranger said.

Scotty followed the stranger to the center of the village where it seemed most everyone was in attendance. Scotty recognized some of the small banana and coconut farmers he had agreements with which made him figure that it wasn't only those in the village that participated in the festival.

A circle had been formed by the villagers and the maidens and drummers made up part of the arc. They sang with enthusiasm and passion for about twenty minutes. Then after a moment of silence the drummers beat out four high volume beats and a lady literally jumped into the middle of the circle and posed there for all to see her brilliance and beauty. She was adorned with colored cloths of yellow, red, blue, and green. She wore a beaded choker that looked like it was made of pearls and diamonds. Her fingernails and toenails were painted a bright red and atop her head sat a crown bedazzled with jewels that matched the colors of her dress. All this was set against the backdrop of ebony skin that had a luster and glow.

After she was satisfied that the crowd was duly impressed, she pointed at the drummers and they began to beat out a different rhythm than before and they were soon joined by a chant from the young soprano maidens whose words were not Spanish but from a language Scotty did not recognize. The Conga Queen swayed to the music, and then rushed from one part of the circle to the other and as she came close to the circle all the male onlookers would stick out their hand hoping the Conga Queen would pick them as the one man who was worthy and be the one pulled into her world.

But no hand did she grab. Some of the braver men would jump into the circle and do a dance circling the Conga Queen but she ignored his presence. After several rebuffs the man would retreat into the crowd defeated. This happened several times and Scotty felt the pain of the defeated man for reasons he could not comprehend.

At first Scotty thought he was imagining things. The Conga Queen stopped her dancing as did the drum and music and she walked straight in the direction of Scotty. She stuck out her hand. He placed his white palm onto the light brown palm of the extended ebony hand and followed her as she gently took him to the middle of the circle. He knew what he was doing, he was not hypnotized or mesmerized, he was just doing what he felt was the natural thing to do under the circumstances while all the time realizing it was not really natural at all, as if he had no choice. She put her arms around Scotty and pressed him close. He put his arms around her. The singers and drummers began a low pitched sound and the drums beat an easy rhythm. Scotty and the Conga Queen swayed gently and moved to the edge of the circle and as it parted the villagers bowed and the couple slid silently into the jungle night.

The next morning Scotty was awoken by the dispatch rider. He handed Scotty a telegram. It read: "You are hereby relieved of duty stop return to senior headquarters immediately stop you did a good job stop. Cavanaugh."

Scotty had little memory of the night before. It seemed more like a dream than reality. He thought it was strange that he would encounter the Conga Queen and the very next day be instructed to leave Nombre. He reluctantly packed. He liked the village, the people, especially Mama Niambi but in his heart knew it was time to go home. His adventure was complete and his mission done, but he could not put into words what sort of adventure he had completed or what mission was accomplished. He would leave with the dispatch rider and not look back. He would take memories forward but a piece of him would always be a part of Nombre de Dios.

CHAPTER 5
Ron McShane

In the middle of the 1920s, Wyoming and Montana each had a U. S. Army Cavalry Regiment. They were extremely tenacious, combative and competitive with one another.

Every year the two regiments would engage in a field training exercise to practice and hone their skills and try to embarrass the other. It was in the Wyoming regiment that Ron McShane found himself.

Ron had left home under less than desirable conditions. He reluctantly joined the Army because there was little else a 16 year old could do with no education or job and no hope of getting either. He saw a recruiting poster in Kansas City, lied about his age to an old grumpy recruiting sergeant and joined up. It was towards the end of the month and there was one slot that needed to be filled and that was for a cook with Troop F of the 5th Wyoming Regimental Horse Cavalry. Ron thought that might not end up being a bad idea. At least he would get plenty to eat and who knew? Maybe he would learn a trade he could use when he left the Army.

Ron reported as ordered and was given the job title and responsibilities as Third Cook. His duties consisted of helping the first cook, second cook and anything the big boss, Mess Sergeant Anderson wanted him to do. He really started at the bottom of the bottom when it came to Army mess hall operations but it was a blessing in disguise. Being a young man hardly into puberty he took everything said to him as gospel and was afraid that if he did not, some dire consequence would befall him. So he was attentive to what he was told and worked very hard at whatever job he was assigned. He became very good at what he did.

One Sunday morning the first and second cooks were so hung over that they could not even begin to go through the motions of preparing the breakfast meal. Mess Sergeant Anderson did not work Sunday mornings and was unaware of the situation. This left Ron in charge.

With the help of two K.P.'s, Acting Mess Sergeant Ron McShane, as he referred to himself that morning, engaged the situation with determination and confidence. Everything did not run smooth as silk that morning but things did not fall apart either. Mess Sergeant Anderson took notice. He had Troop Captain North transfer the first and second cook to permanent stable duty and promoted Ron to First Cook. "Select who you want to assist you," said Anderson.

Ron liked the added responsibility and eventually

became so adept at running the mess hall and field kitchen that Mess Sergeant Anderson started giving Ron more and more responsibilities. Soon Ron was running the whole show while the mess sergeant played golf or spent time at the nearest Indian reservation where he had a common law wife and blood child. Ron did not mind, he was just as glad that the sergeant stayed away. F Troop Commander North did not mind because the troops were well fed and a well fed trooper was a contented trooper and a contented trooper was a good cavalryman.

The mess sergeant eventually retired from the service and Ron was given the job.

'F Troop Mess Sergeant McShane' was the sign he put up on the wall of the private room in the barracks that came with the job. This is all Ron had ever wanted from the first day he arrived at Fort Jackson. Ron was left alone to run the mess hall the best way he thought and his mess section operated flawlessly. He had it operating like a well corn-oiled machine, so to speak. However, a well-intentioned but new and young officer showed up in the troop. He thought that since he was given the extra duty as mess officer he needed to supervise Ron and make sure Ron was doing the job to Army standards.

At first Ron did not mind Lieutenant McVey going over the menus and inspecting food supply requisitions. Nor did he mind a whole lot when McVey started coming in early in the morning to check and see if the cooks were arriving on time. What Ron did mind, however, was when McVey explained to Ron that the yearly field exercise was coming up with the 8th Montana and the newly appointed Colonel of the 5th Wyoming was determined to score better in all areas of tactical and logistical competition than their historical rival; like Ron didn't know this already. McVey was going to make sure that the mess section of Troop F was going to be at its very best. This comment sent Ron over the edge.

Ron told the lieutenant that he need not worry about F Troop mess unless the lieutenant kept coming around annoying the mess sergeant. This caused such an uproar that Lieutenant McVey took Mess Sergeant Ron McShane to the colonel's office and demanded that McShane be court marshaled for insubordination.

Although the 5th Cavalry Commanding Officer was new to his present position he was not new to the 5th Cavalry and knew the reputation of Sergeant McShane. He gave Ron a verbal dressing down and sent him back to the mess hall and then transferred Lieutenant McVey to another Troop.

It was the fourth day into the two week field exercise competition between the 5th and the 8th Cavalry. Things were pretty close, their scores were tied and none of the evaluators could find one thing wrong with unit tactics or individual soldiering skills, mounted and dismounted, used by either cavalry. More emphasis the evaluators decided was going to be placed on combat support maneuvering and necessary logistical support methods in delivering supplies to the front line. They were going to look for innovative and creative techniques.

Setting up, taking down, and moving a field kitchen is no small task. There are stoves to move, fires to start and extinguish, wagons to load and unload, tents to erect and take down and men to feed. Although Ron and his mess section were expert in doing all the above, Ron thought there must be a better and more efficient way of feeding the troops.

During a mess staff meeting Ron came up with an idea. Instead of the mess section accompanying the troop wherever they went he would establish a central point for the field kitchen. That being the case, instead of the mess kitchen personnel trying to find the troops, Ron would detach to the maneuvering force a mess wagon and driver. The troop commander would then send the wagon to the rear area mess as the tactical situation allowed and not be concerned with the mess section slowing them down.

Troop F was given a mission to patrol an area of the border between Wyoming and Montana. The area they were responsible for was about 20 miles in length. They were to ensure that no member of the 8th Cavalry crossed that line without being detected. Ron decided this would be the ideal time to implement his plan. He did not get permission from the higher-ups. It was his mess kitchen and his troops that needed feeding and it was just as well that a bunch of desk jockeys back at headquarters did not interfere.

Ron selected a spot near the middle of the 20 mile front line two miles to the rear. He set up his field kitchen and organized his staff in such a manner so they could prepare meals and have food available 24 hours a day. He sent one wagon and cook to the line being guarded and told him to return and get food as directed by the troop commander.

The troop commander and his officers embraced the idea because they did not have to provide security for the cumbersome mobile mess kitchen, the men did not have to be relieved in shifts to eat and food was available at any time. The quality of the meals improved given the competition between the shifts doing the cooking. Besides morale was high and the men were content and well fed. A contented troop makes a good cavalryman and several good cavalrymen make a good Troop.

The evaluators noticed that Troop F had fewer infiltrators coming from Montana than Montana had coming from Wyoming. They commended the Troop F Commander.

In an after-action report the F Troop Commander made the comment that he attributed most of the success in guarding the border to the diligence, concentration and morale of his men. "They performed their duties without concerning themselves with creature comforts. Much credit must be given to Mess Sergeant Ronald McShane in devising a method of providing meals to the troops on demand."

The 5th Cavalry outscored the 8th that year and at the awards ceremony Mess Sergeant McShane was duly recognized and was presented with the Army Commendation Medal.

After the ceremony the 5th Regimental Cavalry commander took Ron aside and told him he was proud of Ron's accomplishment but he wished there was some way the men out in the field could have gotten eggs to order each morning.

"Sir," Ron responded with a salute, "The men got eggs to order every morning, I ordered scrambled."

Chapter 6
Elroy McShane

Elroy McShane was from a branch of the
McShane's that had settled in northern Indiana.
The family had been farmers in Pennsylvania and
then after the Revolutionary War when the new
government started giving veterans plots of land out
west, one of the cousins of Jonas McShane, Arthur
McShane, jumped at the chance. The McShanes
of Indiana had been farmers for as long as anyone
could remember. The McShanes of the 1930s had
no knowledge of the McShanes of bygone years.
They were farmers, those rugged individuals that
would harness and feed a nation. Over the years
they had amassed enough land to let each child and
grandchild have a quarter section upon reaching the
age of twenty-one.

The family was put into a quandary however when
Elroy McShane told his father and grandfather that
he did not want to be a farmer and that he intended
to sell his portion of the land to one of his brothers.
That was something no McShane in memory had
ever done.

"What do you plan on doing with your life then?" asked Grandpa McShane.

"With my life I don't know, but for the next few months or so I plan on riding the rails and see some place other than Hope County, Indiana," was Elroy's reply.

Elroy first went to Detroit but found the city too congested. He then went to Chicago where things were more congested but he was running out of money so he took a day job at a meat packing plant. The conditions and the way they treated the animals disgusted him and even though jobs were almost impossible to find he jumped into the first empty boxcar heading west.

He would stop now and then, find work for a day or two and hear from the growing hobo population that he was becoming part of that there was some work to be had at such and such a location. He would hop a train or hitch a ride to see for himself.

He had no ties, no responsibilities, and no timetable to keep like many men during that time in America. Some were bums but most of them who traveled the rails were schooled, if not well-educated, decent people who were pursuing something but what it was exactly kept evading them.

Elroy, who had a high school diploma, learned a lot more from the hobos he met along the way. The stories he heard around the camp fire many a night did nothing but keep him interested in exploring what he was beginning to realize was a huge and diverse country, his land.

Elroy liked Hope County, Indiana but he fell in
love with America. He realized how fortunate he
was to live in such a country and after listening to
one hobo one evening about his exploits in the
military, Elroy decided what to do with his life. He
would join the service the first chance he got. In
that way he could serve his country and at the same
time see many things that most in Hope County
never dreamed existed.

After crossing the Rocky Mountains his first stop
was Cheyenne, Wyoming where he immediately
sought out an Army recruiter. He signed the papers
and was sent to the nearest military induction
center, which just so happened to be down the
street two blocks. There he found out that he was
unfit for military service because he had flat feet and
was absent his right index finger due to a farming
accident. "Son, you can't walk far and can't fire
a gun, you are no use to the Army," the medical
examiner told him.

Elroy was crushed. He had built up in his mind
a life in the Army and the adventures he would be
having. He saw himself returning to Hope County
with a chest full of medals and riding as the grand
marshal in the Harvest Parade. He was really in a
stupor.

He continued his journey but with no real
objective. He saw the Grand Canyon but was
unimpressed, Yellowstone National Park thrilled
him not, and the Redwood Forest of northern

California left him uninspired. He was about to give up and return to Hope County and work the farm. Perhaps he could get his quarter section after all.

It was only when he viewed the Pacific Ocean near San Francisco and saw a ship pass by and sail out of sight did it occur to him that he might be able to join the United States Navy. Sailors did not have to walk a lot nor were they expected to fire a gun. What they did do he was not sure but he did know how to swim so surely that must be a plus for joining the Navy. He was wrong. The Navy would not have him either and for the same reasons. Elroy protested and pointed out to the doctor since the Navy did not do a lot of walking or shoot a lot of guns he did not understand why he was being rejected. Personally, the doctor agreed with him but regulations were regulations and had to be followed.

The doctor had seen many a man like Elroy. He always hated turning young men down but Navy regulations were not the same as Coast Guard regulations since the Coast Guard was part of the Department of Commerce. The doctor knew a recruiter for the Coast Guard who said he could always use a good man. The doctor sent Elroy to see him.

Elroy had not even heard of the Coast Guard but the recruiter made a good pitch and Elroy joined. The flat feet and absent trigger finger made no difference.

Elroy was assigned as third mate to a Coast Guard cutter that patrolled the waters between Seattle and

Anchorage. He became an able bodied seaman and rose through the ranks quickly. There was just enough adventure in being in the Coast Guard to keep one's interest high and monotony low. There was always some fool that capsized his boat and needed rescuing, smugglers that needed chasing and ships needing searches for contraband.

One winter there was a week layover in Anchorage. The cutter's captain assembled the men and told them that their ship had been given the task of supplying typhoid vaccine to a village called Wilson Bay located on the western edge of Alaska. Regional tribal leaders would gather in Wilson Bay and distribute the vaccine to the villages and isolated camps in the area. There was too much vaccine needed for a plane to carry and the current and foreseeable weather conditions were not good for flying. Their ship could make it just fine as long as they could get there and back before the pack ice formed and the Bering Sea became more treacherous than normal.

The only danger was that at this time of year and in that part of the world weather conditions could change in an instant. If the cutter were trapped in the ice all aboard would have to somehow manage to live till the thaw. "The ship will not be caught in the ice, under any circumstances," the captain announced.

The captain told the Coast Guardsmen that he was only going to take a skeleton crew due to the danger and wanted volunteers. Every man aboard volunteered. Elroy was one of the men selected.

Right before leaving Elroy wrote his mother and father and told them what was happening. He wrote that he was proud to be a member of the Coast Guard and felt privileged to be selected for the mission he was about to undertake with a group of men who he had served with for over a year now. If anything happened to him he wanted his quarter section that Grandpa McShane refused to let anyone else use until his grandson's return, to be divided equally with his brothers.

The first part of the voyage was easy enough but as they rounded Bethel the sea became choppier and the wind grew stronger. Elroy had never been seasick before but he made up for it on that trip. The first day after rounding Bethel he thought he would die and the second day he was afraid he would not. Finally, on the third day the sea settled down enough that he got his strength and sea-legs back and was able to carry out his duties.

The ship's captain assembled the crew and told them they were five miles off the western coast of Alaska and that Wilson Bay was iced in and they could go no further by ship. He said the vaccine would have to be transported by foot over the pack ice. Each man looked out over the ship's aft and immediately noticed that walking on pack ice was not like walking on a frozen pond. There were chunks of ice protruding upwards through a frozen sea and whose tips were jagged and pointed. They formed sharp edges that had to be gone over or around. Some of the ice took on a bluish tint which puzzled everyone aboard and now and then the ice seemed to flatten out and look as smooth as a skating rink and had a greenish tint.

The ship's executive officer said that although polar bears did not usually come this far south, it was always possible and each man was to carry a rifle. "Except for you, Seaman Elroy," and all assembled laughed at the inside joke.

Because of the danger the captain again asked for volunteers. Every man aboard did so and half were selected. Elroy was one of them. The captain told the men that the ship could only wait two days for them to return. The weather forecast warned of icing further out from the coast and all Coast Guard ships and boats were to be at a longitude and latitude that was predicted by the National Weather Service not to freeze over. The captain felt no remorse in abandoning the men if necessary. If they did get stranded in Wilson Bay there was enough shelter and supplies to last until a plane could be sent and he was positive the native Eskimos would assist them in any way possible.

The men journeyed east on the ice. The going was arduous and dangerous. The tops of the pack ice that had been thrust up due to compression were as sharp as any razor. The packs of medicine seemed to grow heavier and heavier while their legs turned to clay. Because of all the zigging and zagging, the five miles easily became ten and a compass reading still put them five miles away when the 15 hours of dark settled in. They all huddled together with their arms around each other trying to absorb their companions' body heat. They did not want to make a fire for fear of melting the ice but then laughed at their own naiveté after realizing there was nothing to burn.

At first light they set off again and had only gone a mile or so when in the distance they saw several sleds pulled by dogs heading their way. The Yupik Eskimos of Wilson Bay somehow knew they were out there on the ice and came to help the men and the precious vaccine make it to the village.

After delivering the vaccine to the small medical dispensary manned by a Jesuit Priest each man was assigned a family to stay with that evening. The family would feed them, keep them warm, and were so thankful for the medicine would provide anything else the men desired.

Before being shown to their host families the executive officer who had accompanied the men wanted a short meeting. He told them not to get to "familiar" with "our friends." Being a devout Quaker the young executive officer could not bring himself to state the obvious. He said he was going to stay with the priest and if any of the men wanted to volunteer to do the same he would be welcomed and room would be made somehow. No one volunteered.

Three days passed and a radio message was sent advising that a plane was being sent to pick up the men who were stranded. No one other than the executive officer wanted to leave Wilson Bay, not even Elroy.

As the men were loading onto the plane the pilot informed the executive officer that due to weather conditions and weight restrictions one man would have to be left behind. The X.O. asked for volunteers and all did. Elroy was selected to stay for at least another day.

The weather immediately turned bad after takeoff and it was three weeks before a plane returned to pick up Elroy. Elroy was reluctant to leave Wilson Bay. He had formed many a close friendship, especially with one young girl. He vowed to return as soon as he could and he meant it but like most young men thrust into an alien environment he never did. Elroy was not the first non-Yupik to pass through Wilson Bay and received the favors of the village, nor would he be the last. The Eskimos of Wilson Bay took such things and relationships in stride. Elroy carried the memory of his time in Wilson Bay the rest of his life and even into old age would wonder what became of the young Eskimo girl he had known and could never shake the feeling that he had left something behind in Wilson Bay, which in fact he had.

CHAPTER 7
Frank McShane

While his distant cousin Elroy, whom he knew nothing of, was delivering typhoid vaccine and getting to know the Yupik Eskimo people first hand in all ways imaginable, Frank McShane was busy getting ready to rotate back to the States from his tour in Hawaii. He had joined the Army six years earlier because there were no jobs in 1935, or at least none that he was interested in doing. He was still living at home and his father finally told him he was either going to get a job on his own or go to work for the family tanning company as an entry level procurement officer. Neither sounded very interesting to Frank.

Uncle Scotty suggested he look into joining the Army like he did but had to admit to Frank he might not be as lucky as he had been with his assignment in Panama. But he reminded Frank that since there was not a war going on and one didn't seem to be in the offing the Army might not be a bad place to be for a few years while he figured things out. "At least you will get three hots and a cot and not have to go into the family business," Scotty told him.

The St. Louis McShanes had no political pull in those days so getting a straight commission as a procurement officer was out of the question. However, Scotty did know an old drinking buddy who had a son that had just been assigned as an Army recruiter and thought he could get Frank a plum assignment.

Frank met with the sergeant and described what he was looking for, which somewhat was the same thing his uncle had fallen into. The sergeant said he could not guarantee that but he did have an opening as an assistant supply clerk at an outpost in the Hawaiian Island chain. "I really don't know a whole lot about the place you would be assigned but I did spend a week in Honolulu delivering parts to the Air Force base once. It was a pretty good place. I would apply for the posting myself but my rank will not allow it now. With your high school ROTC training I think I can get basic training waived. That is if you sign up now." Frank signed up.

Two months later Frank got off a ship at a little island at the very west of the Hawaiian Island chain called Kawaniwa. Kawaniwa was the location of an Army Air Force field called Last Stop. The Army had selected that particular location as a weather station. For the protection of the weather station the Army had assigned a company of United State Infantry from the 25th Division.

For the 120 men counting "clerks and jerks" there was supposed to be a supply sergeant and supply clerk. For some reason known only to an Army personnel clerk somewhere in the basement of the War Department, the clerk position was never filled.

The company commander, Captain Farris, of Company A as the Infantry unit was so designated, never really saw the need for a supply clerk. The current supply sergeant said a new man would be more trouble training than it would be worth. It wasn't until the supply sergeant announced he was retiring did Captain Farris decide they might want to fill the clerk position soon so the job could be learned and there be no break in supply operations. So enters Private Frank McShane.

Sergeant First Class Pete Jenson had been in the Army for almost 20 years and most of them had been in Hawaii. He had a little bungalow just a few miles from the gate that housed his Hawaiian wife and three beautiful daughters, all under the age of 10 he would remind all the young men who asked about his girls.

Frank learned the paper work quickly. The ordering of supplies was little different than procuring items at the family business.

Since Pete was retiring soon he and Frank spent much time with each other and got on a first name basis. Pete taught Frank the ins and outs of the Army supply business that was not found in any technical manual. "One of the most important aspects of the system," Pete lectured Frank, "was in the way you account for items under your direct control. Always keep things locked up and never let anything outside the supply room without someone signing a receipt indicating that they now are in possession of the item. That way when an inspection takes place you either have the item or a piece of paper that tells the inspector that someone else has the item. The item may never show up again but at least it won't be your fault and no one can make you pay for it."

"However," continued Pete, "Even with a keen eye and diligent record keeping you will count and recount the items and somehow they will not match the inventory you are supposed to have. That is when you get creative. Any time there is a field exercise there are bound to be losses through normal use and wear and tear. On most items that is around 1 to 3 percent Army-wide, but that is statistically speaking. I have never had that much. So if you have a hundred men participating in a field exercise, that means that you can drop 1 to 3 percent of your items from your inventory and replace them with a requisition. Then if you get inspected before you receive the requisitioned item you will have the paper to cover you. If you get the items before any inspection you just put them aside somewhere out of the way and when an item comes up missing on your weekly count you just replace it with the overages you have accumulated over time."

"Fine system," said Frank. "How much overage do you normally keep on hand?"

"I have enough of everything that an infantry-sized unit like Company A would need twice. In fact, I am running out of room and really don't know what I am going to do with the excess," Pete responded. Pete then took Frank to the other side of the island and showed him a medium thatched stone hut full of tents, sleeping bags, blankets, boots, clothes and all other sorts of items that an individual soldier would need.

"I don't see any weapons, ammunition, and things like that," Frank said.

"Nor will you. That sort of thing could get a man in trouble quick. No one really cares about tents and stuff like that but when you start fooling around with rifles and such, it is a one-way ticket to Leavenworth." Pete lectured.

Frank took heed to what Pete said and continued to maintain order and stay on top of the supply situation when Pete mustered out. He and the Company A Commander were always given an outstanding rating whenever a battalion or division inspection occurred.

A tour in the Army has different effects on people. Sometimes they go in with a chip on their shoulder and come out the same way. Sometimes they go in full of piss and vinegar and come out deflated. Some go in not knowing what to expect and end up finding something they are good at and take pride in doing the job and enjoy the praise. It might be for the first time in their life such a thing had happened to them and they like the feeling. They hope they can keep doing it when they get out of the Army. Frank fell under that category and he had a job waiting.

Although Frank liked the Army he was ready to come home. Six years was enough. He wrote his father and asked if he could take a job in the family business and asked if he could start at the bottom as a tanner and learn every aspect of the company. He said he wanted to run the company someday and knew he could use the skills and tools he had received in the Army to the family firm's advantage.

He was scheduled to depart Hawaii in one week, which would be December 13, but he wanted to send some packages home first so they would be sure to arrive around the same time he would. He mailed everything on December 6th and went to bed that night excited about spending the Christmas of 1941with his friends and family.

CHAPTER 8
Allen McShane

If there ever was a McShane that did not want
to serve in the military in any fashion whatsoever,
peacetime or not, it was Allen McShane, son of Ron,
who was the mess sergeant for Troop F. Allen liked
Wyoming and saw no reason to leave it and scurry
about the world fighting other peoples' battles. If he
had been old enough to participate in World War II
he would have gone, of course. That was different -
this thing in Korea made no sense to him at all.

Allen married his high school sweetheart and
they had a baby six months later, so when the
draft started in earnest to fill the depleted ranks
of those who left the service after WW II, he was
exempt. However, two years after the baby came,
his high school sweetheart went. He was never
sure who informed the draft board or if they just
automatically found out about such things but it
wasn't two months after the divorce was final that he
received his 1A classification in the mail.

He requested a deferment due to his having single
parent custody and thus the responsibility of raising

his child. The president of the Selective Service Board contacted the child's mother to see what she had to say and she informed the board president that Allen didn't even have joint custody of the child and besides that, he was late on his first child support payment. Allen's ex asked the nice lady if there was anything the Selective Service could do to insure that child support payments be paid in a timely manner. The nice lady told her no, not really, but she knew someone who could. Two days later Allen received his draft notice.

Allen reported to Camp Roberts in northern California for basic training. To his surprise he really didn't mind at all. Being from Wyoming he had spent a lot of time in the outdoors camping, hunting, and fishing and was already in good physical condition. He didn't like being told what to do though and thought many of his fellow soldiers were immature which was true. The average age in his basic training company was 19 and Allen was 24, but basic training had a way of bringing a diverse group into a cohesive one. By the time basic was completed he never thought he would have any better friends than he had right then. He still did not enjoy being in the military - not minding being there and liking being there were two different things.

As orders were being handed out most everyone was expecting to be sent to Korea. Allen was pleasantly surprised when he received orders for the advanced school for cooks that the Navy ran in San Diego. He thought he might just follow in his father's footsteps and, better yet, avoid going to Korea.

There were ten men in that particular training cycle at Camp Roberts who received similar orders. The orders were followed up that same day by a visit from each man's company commander telling him to check in all their field gear except clothing and a duffel bag. Any personal clothing was to be packed along with their military clothing in the one duffel and each man was told to report to the brigade headquarters at midnight. All were told not to write or call anyone and tell them about their orders until they arrived at their destination.

It was an all night and half a day's trip from Camp Roberts to the San Diego Naval Yard. The men were dropped off at what was to become their barracks for the next few weeks and told not to leave the area.

The next morning the men were loaded onto a five ton truck and taken to the mess hall that served the officers. They were unloaded at the back of the building and climbed an outside set of stairs to a classroom and were told to sit and wait. Within a few minutes a short man with horn-rimmed glasses, flat top and business suit came into the room and situated himself in front of the men.

"Gentlemen," he began, "this is not an advanced cook school run by the Navy. This is a school for soldiers who have a higher than normal probability of being captured and imprisoned by the enemy.

I say that because statistics show that men who served in certain sectors of the front line in Korea, which is where you will be sent, had a higher than average occurrence of being taken prisoner. This is not a volunteer assignment or school because no one is asking you to become a POW. But if you do, however, there are certain things we want you to do while imprisoned that will help ensure your survival and help your country as well. We want you to write letters home."

Allen and the other men mumbled under their breath to each other sort of nondescript sounds that each understood to be, "What is this guy talking about?"

Like the man in front could read their minds he said, "What I am talking about is that if captured we want you to tell us – your family – what is going on in the prison camps. Gentlemen, we have less information coming out of the North Korean POW camps than we have ever had in any other war. We know there are plenty of POWs but the information we receive through letters exchanged for us by the Red Cross have very little information that we can use for intelligence purposes. You will be taught a code, a cipher, and you will send letters to a fictitious family member. This family member may even be a girl friend you intend on marrying when you get home. You two will write each other coded letters. Asking and answering information that will be used by military intelligence. I probably don't need to say this but I must, you are never to talk to anyone when outside this room about what goes on in this room, not even to each other. When you are given the name of the family member or girlfriend, you are not to reveal that identity to anyone ever. Are there any questions? If not, your first assignment is to learn this poem," and he started reciting.

The poem was quite lengthy and the meter awkward. It took each man in the room more than a week working several hours a day to memorize the work of the poet none of them had ever heard about. At the end of the first week each man had to stand in front of the group and recite the poem. If he made a mistake he had to start all over again. It took two weeks for all the men to recite the poem verbatim. Until the end of their training the poem would be recited in unison each morning before the day's instruction was to begin.

The cipher was based on the date the letter was written and in which corner the date was located. It was also important if the date and/or letter itself was written in cursive or printed. The way the date was displayed was an indication as to the numbering sequence the first sentence of the letter was to have. The numbers would be added and then applied to the poem. It was a complicated process and more than one of the men, including Allen, thought they would never be able to master the technique.

The Army and the military in general had pioneered instructional techniques that made the most difficult if not comprehensible at least learnable. Each man did learn the procedure and each man graduated from the secret school with a secret attachment in his personnel file that would physically be kept under lock and key by the Federal Bureau of Investigation. None of the men knew it at the time but that tag on their security jacket would follow them the rest of their lives and resurface now and then.

The men were sent back to Camp Roberts and split into ten different units all waiting transport to Korea. Allen still did not want to be in the Army and especially did not want to be captured but he was a realist and thought he might as well make the best of things. Besides there was still talk about the war winding down and just before he arrived a cease fire had been negotiated.

Allen's company boarded a troop ship called the USS Mann and two weeks later was let off at a place called Enchoy. At Enchoy his company climbed aboard several two and a half ton trucks and taken to their base camp called Zone 37. Allen was assigned a tent with six other men and made a squad leader of an infantry platoon. At mail call the next morning Allen received a letter from his "girlfriend" Marsha, who lived at 221 Main Street, Sweet Springs, Wyoming. Sweet Springs was only 20 miles from his home in Casper.

He immediately deciphered the letter. She wanted to know how the trip over was, and if he liked his tent mates and that they needed to keep in practice if they ever had to use his training for real.

She said that she would write him once a month and he was to respond. Allen answered back that he understood and would comply.

The year he was supposed to be in Korea went by quicker than Allen had thought it would. In spite of himself, he enjoyed much of his time there. Oddly enough, he would run across more than just a few boys from his neighborhood; strange he thought being so far away and all. But when he thought about it, it wasn't that odd at all. Most everyone he knew had been drafted or joined the Army and most of them had been sent to Korea. The front line in Korea was not very long and the divisions were packed very close together. He even ran into his family doctor who had stayed in the reserves after WW II and gotten called up.

He spent most of his time on guard duty which could be boring and usually was. However, now and then something of interest would occur. One day he heard a man yelling for help down by the docks that happened to be near his guard post. Allen checked the situation out and saved the man from drowning. It turned out to be a North Korean trying to infiltrate the camp for sabotage but forgot to tell his handlers in the north he couldn't swim. Allen was awarded the Bronze Star and a V for valor.

Once Allen's captain got irritated that there was no sugar in the mess hall and that battalion supply was not allowing his cooks to requisition it due to some "stupid military regulation, no doubt," the captain growled. The company commander told

Allen to get a jeep and two MPs and meet him in front of company headquarters.

The company commander jumped in the front seat of the waiting jeep with two MPs in the back seat and Allen behind the wheel. "Find me the nearest whore house," the captain barked.

Allen didn't really know where one was but one of the MPs did. Allen parked out front of the 'Madam Shang' while the two MPs and the captain went inside the building and within a few minutes came out with several five pound sugar bags being carried by one of the MPs. The other MP had the battalion supply sergeant in tow. "Sometimes you just get lucky," the captain said. After a short talk to the handcuffed supply sergeant he was let go and the mess hall and MP post never went without sugar or any other food commodities again.

Allen got a furlough for two weeks so he went to Tokyo where he met a "nice girl" he wrote his mother in Casper. She was a nice girl but the romance only lasted for two letters after he returned to Zone 37 which had been named Base Camp HST after the former president.

Allen was not a fan of the Koreans as a people but as individuals he found them to be kind and generous. The men of his company might be hard on Korean civilians who worked around the base but these same men adopted a young Korean boy they found hiding in a ship down by the docks. The men would write home and tell their parents to send them jackets and clothes so the young man, all of ten years old, would have adequate clothing. The response was immediate and plentiful. Allen didn't wait to hear from home so he went to the Division PX and bought the boy a jacket that would face any severe weather Korea could throw their way. They let the boy sleep in their tents next to the oil burning stove. He was like a mascot.

One day a Catholic missionary priest came into camp because he had heard about the boy. He said he was there to take the boy to the Catholic orphanage in Seoul. The men made subtle and not so subtle threats that they would check up on the boy periodically and if he was not well taken care of some one would regret it mightily.

Allen still did not like being in the Army but due to attrition of personnel and seniority, towards the end of his enlistment he was a Sergeant First Class and had less than two months left in Korea and three months left in the Army. He had it counted down to the wire.

During his 'out processing' his interviewer said that if he would sign up for just three more months in Korea he would send Allen to military flight school where he would learn how to fly helicopters. Helicopters had intrigued Allen ever since he had seen his first one at Camp Roberts. He would have to re-enlist for three years, however, if the flight school paper work went through. It was tempting. He had no idea what he was going to do when he got out of the service. The recruiter did say that he did not have to make up his mind right then but had up to two months after termination of service to rejoin and apply for helicopter school.

Allen wanted to go home. He wanted to see his son and the rest of his family. He even thought that there might be a possibility of him and his former wife getting back together. They had been corresponding and both would write things in the letters that should have been said sooner and much could be read between the lines. Maybe it might work this time, he thought. Both had matured over the last two years.

Allen received a letter from Marsha one week before he was to rotate home. In it for all the world to read, she said that it had been nice corresponding with him this last year but she had a new boyfriend now and did not think it fair to him to keep writing a soldier. The coded part of the letter was, 'your mission is accomplished, do not respond to this letter and make no attempt to contact me.'

Allen arrived home on Sunday morning, had Sunday dinner with his mother, father and son, and even his former wife stopped by for dessert. Monday morning he had the oil changed in his car, his tires checked, filled the old Chevrolet up with gas and drove to Sweet Springs, Wyoming. He found Main Street and went in the direction of 221 and found that there was no 221 Main Street.

Allen got back in his car and drove back to Casper, went to the Army recruiting station and asked how much would a Sergeant First Class make with two dependents and how much money would he receive in flight pay if he became a pilot.

CHAPTER 9
Eloy McShane

Eloy scanned the snow-capped ice as far as the Army issued binoculars would allow. Having satisfied himself that nothing was afoot on the horizon, he moved on to a different sector. He would cover ten sectors that day on skis and snowshoes when skiing was impossible due to the pack ice.

Eloy was the product of what the natives referred to as 'Sailors blood.' It was a term handed down from the whaling days when European whaling ships would anchor just off shore to barter and trade with the coastal Eskimos. Most villages were so isolated then that inbreeding and the resulting consequences were recognized by the villagers. When a ship arrived off shore the seamen, some of whom had been at sea for a year, traded almost anything they had for what the Eskimos had plenty of. There was no shame in any of this and it was looked on as a natural way of preserving the healthiness of the tribe.

Old habits die hard and when in modern time

a Gussick, any non Eskimo, lived with or close to a tribe, things just took a natural course. Eloy's biological father was Elroy McShane, who helped save the village from a typhoid epidemic - Elroy had no idea that Eloy existed. Eloy's uncle, brother to his mother, helped raise Eloy. Uncles traditionally took on such roles whether or not the father was part of the household. The uncle taught Eloy the art of surviving in the Arctic.

Eloy loved his village of Wilson Bay. It was not hard for him to make the decision to join the Territorial Scout Battalion that would act as an early warning system and the front line of defense if the Soviet Union decided to launch a land invasion across the Bering Straits. There were hundreds of the Eskimo Scouts guarding the border during the early part of the Cold War. The Army thought it was a good 'bang for the buck' because most of the Eskimo Scouts only wanted a rifle, winter supplies and ammunition.

Each village was assigned a large area to observe and it was the chief's job to ensure that the area be divided into sectors and monitored daily. The chief sought out seven of the strongest and the smartest and made them responsible for monitoring the sections one day a week. He also had an eighth person to fill in just in case of sickness. The young men eagerly accepted the chief's request, especially when told they could use their rifle to hunt for game when not on duty.

Ten forward observation posts were established

along a line established by the military. These huts or igloos could also be used for shelter if a storm came upon the men suddenly. They were not intended to sleep in otherwise. The Wilson Bay scouts did begin stocking the igloos with dried fish and fruit just in case the storm lasted any length of time and they were stranded for a few days.

Eloy was good at his job and even better providing for his wife, son called Shane, his mother and grandmother and two aunts. He never went out on a patrol or a hunt that he did not bring back something to eat; it could be a seal, bird or fish. Life was good.

One day a white man came to the village and informed the Eskimo Scouts that they no longer had to observe the border but would need to keep their rifles as a first line of defense just in case the Russians did attack. Their sectors would now be monitored by radar stations erected at overlapping intervals and make for twenty-four hour, seven days a week coverage all year round. They said that radar technicians would live in selected villages.

The elders shook their head knowingly. It was about time more sailor blood was brought into the village. The young men like Eloy did not think the same way and set out to protect the young women and even their own wives against what they thought would be an onslaught of white man aggression.

Nothing could have been further from the truth. The technicians brought with them their wives and young children; after them followed school teachers whose job it was to train the more talented Eskimos in the art of teaching and eventually replace the white teachers altogether. The radar technicians had the same charge from the government: they were to teach the young men how to operate, repair and monitor the equipment.

Eloy observed what was happening. He was conflicted. In one respect the village and his people would be better off with the increased money and knowledge flowing into the village but in another respect his village would be no more. He had already noticed that many of the young, even his son Shane, were interested in what was happening in places that had nothing to do with Wilson Bay. Eventually, the young would leave the village.

Things were changing and there would be no going back. But then he reasoned there never is or was a going back once the sailors come ashore or the young women ventured out to the ships.

CHAPTER 10
Baylor McShane

It was 1967; the Viet Nam War was still raging with no end in sight. Baylor was never concerned about the rightness or wrongness of the war. He, like most of his friends, liked the life they were living and believed the government knew more than they did and was doing what it should be doing in Southeast Asia.

They had grown up with ducking and covering and believed the threat of Communism was real and just around the corner and the military should do all it could to prevent the Russians from crossing the Mississippi River. Of course, the military consisted of others, not them. It was not that any of the guys Baylor ran around with were opposed to the war but none wanted to go either. Any thoughts they had about not wanting to be drafted and sent to Viet Nam were based more on not wanting to get shot and possibly killed than on ideology.

Being called a draft dodger would have made any of them bristle. In their minds there was a difference between dodging the draft and avoiding the draft as long as you could. They all suspected they would eventually get drafted and they wanted to postpone the inevitable as long as possible. No one he knew ever considered going to Canada, which was the ultimate draft avoidance technique. There were other methods short of that that were acceptable to most of America, though.

Some Americans opposed the war based on religious beliefs and sought Conscientious Objector status. The Quakers could fall into this category but many chose to serve anyway. The Mormons were given a two-year exemption from the draft when they graduated high school if they went on their two-year mission.

Some young men joined one of the other branches of service. They did so under the assumption that more Army and Marines were sent to Viet Nam than were Navy, Air Force, and Coast Guard members, which was true.

Some could not pass the physical. Most were just unfit while others tried to manipulate the system so they would receive the 4F designation. Some were successful and some were not. One of the guys in the neighborhood had hurt his knee years earlier. When he reported to his pre-induction physical he brought with him a handful of documents and x-rays, a cane and pronounced limp. He was on the bus to Fort Leonard Wood that evening. Another guy well known in the neighborhood would gain a lot of weight right before his physical and be flunked by the doctors for being obese. He was told to lose weight and he would be notified when to return for a follow-up examination. He would return home, lose the weight and when he got notice to reappear he would gain the weight all over again. He did this several times. Eventually the authorities gave in and stopped sending him notices.

If one planned far enough ahead he was able to join the National Guard. There were few National Guard units activated to fight the Viet Nam War. If one was able to get a slot in the National Guard he was likely never to be put in harm's way. There were long waiting lists for every National Guard Unit in the country.

Baylor and most of his friends did what many a male did back then - they went to college and got a 2S deferment. Those were guaranteed tickets not to get drafted, at least for four years. All one had to do was remain a student in good standing - meaning passing the number of college credit hours necessary to remain a full time student each semester. Therein lay the rub for Baylor.

Baylor had enrolled at the local junior college to raise his grade point average so he could return to the college he had flunked out of and try to regain a squandered athletic scholarship. That semester, he took eighteen hours, dropped eight and flunked two. That made him short of the number of hours necessary to qualify for the 2S exemption status.

He thought he needed to do something quickly before the junior college had time to send his name to the local draft board and they, in turn, change his status to 1A. Having had student deferments for two years made him feel like he would probably be priority draft and whisked off to some God-forsaken military basic training center. He really didn't know what to do.

This is when the real funk started; some might call it depression. He was not going to school, the junior college wouldn't even let him back in and his last girlfriend had just dumped him because she said he had no ambition. She then up and married a divinity school graduate who was going into the Coast Guard as a Chaplin.

Feeling sorry for himself and in a complete quandary, he drove by the junior college. He decided to see if anyone was in the student union that he could pass the time with between their classes. As he was entering the student recreational center he noticed a sign on the information bulletin board that read "Do You Want to Beat the Draft?" That caught his attention. He continued to read the sign. "If so report to room 214 at 2 P.M this coming Tuesday and we will show you how." Baylor showed up fifteen minutes early that day.

There were about 10 in the room that morning counting Baylor, all males and one female who said she was taking notes for her boyfriend. There was a man in uniform standing in front of the group who introduced himself as Colonel Darby.

Darby explained the purpose of the gathering and the meaning of the sign that had brought them to the room that afternoon.

"The Central State College is implementing a program in cooperation with the United States Army. If you are eligible you will be able to fulfill your military obligation and complete your education. All the Army requires from you is a commitment to complete an augmented basic training session this summer, which you will be paid to attend and an advanced camp the following summer, for which you will also be financially compensated. Each session lasts six weeks. In addition, during your junior and senior year at college you will be required to take advanced military science classes. When you graduate you will receive a commission in the United States Army as a Second Lieutenant and have a two year obligation to serve full time as an Army officer.

"Every freshman enrolling at CSC next year will be required to take the basic class in the Reserve Officer Training Program, better known as ROTC and be given the option the following year to take the next level to prepare themselves for senior cadre positions. You, having gone through the augmented basic training session this summer, will be accredited with six semester hours which automatically puts you into the Advanced Program where you will act as Senior Cadre for the Cadet Corps.

"To be eligible to participate in this program you have to be a junior in college this coming year, successfully complete the augmented basic training program, and pass an academic entry exam. So as not to waste your time or mine, you will take the test in fifteen minutes. Take a break, think the situation over, and talk amongst yourselves. Those of you who return to this room and take and pass the test will be taken to the administrative offices down the hall to complete the necessary paperwork. Oh, yes, I forgot to mention that as senior cadre you will be paid $50 a month while attending school for the next two years. Any questions? Dismissed."

Several of those attending the meeting gathered outside the entrance to the Junior College. "I could use a job this summer. How hard could it be?" "Fifty dollars a month would really come in handy." "At least there would be two more years for the war to get over." "I guess if you have to go get shot at you might as well get paid better." "You know, that really doesn't sound like a bad idea." Baylor just listened.

In fifteen minutes Darby returned. All but one of the original ten who had shown up earlier and the female who had been taking notes for her boyfriend followed Darby back into the room. "Have a seat gentlemen," Darby said, and started handing out the tests.

They would be given one hour to complete the exam. It would be graded immediately and before they left the room they would know if they had passed or failed. Baylor wondered if the rest of the guys realized this was the most important one hour of their lives.

CHAPTER 11
Aaron McShane

Aaron McShane's family owned a chain of pizza parlors throughout Idaho, Montana and Wyoming called Pizza Slice.   Grandpa Ron started Pizza Slice when he retired from the Cavalry in the early 30's. He more or less brought pizza to the attention of the northwestern cowboy. They found it easy to eat while riding the back country and easy to pack in their saddle bags. Grandpa Ron came up with the idea because one of his first cooks was from New York and was always talking about how he missed "buying a slice."

On the same day that Baylor McShane was reporting to Fort Knox for his augmented basic training, Aaron was graduating from Wyoming University with a degree in economics. One week after that Aaron received his 1A classification with a handwritten note from the president of the selective service office in Cheyenne saying "see you soon."

"Not in this lifetime," Aaron said to himself and one week later he joined the Air Force.

After basic training in Texas, Aaron hoped to be

assigned to a missile administration detachment
in northwest Idaho but instead he was sent to
Davis AFB near the western mouth of the Panama
Canal. He was assigned to a job befitting his
degree in economics – motor pool clerk. It was
his job to check in and check out military vehicles
to authorized personnel. He was also responsible
for the care and upkeep of all the vehicles but
this was easier than it sounded. The E4 he took
over the job from said that he didn't need to go
out and check the oil and wash the vehicles when
the vehicle was returned. "When the vehicle is
returned you inspect the vehicle once and if it is not
up to standard then you refuse to take it until the
using party brings it to you in the same condition
in which they received it. You will be clear with
any inspection team. You will not get a gig as long
as you have the number of vehicles that you are
supposed to have or a receipt from the person who
signed it out." Aaron didn't think the job would
be very difficult. "It even gets better than that," the
airman continued, "Hardly anyone checks a vehicle
in after they check it out. As long as you got the
receipt you are not responsible what happens to
the vehicle or where it goes. You also have the use
of any vehicle in the pool anytime you want. Just
make sure you have a receipt made out to yourself
if an inspector comes by while you are off duty and
using the vehicle."

"How often does an inspection occur?" asked
Aaron.

"I don't know. I have been doing this job for a year now and I have yet to have one. Sometimes I think the higher-ups forget that there is a motor pool. As long as they have their transportation when they want it they don't care where it comes from."

Aaron and the E4 airman made a count of the vehicles in the motor pool and counted the number of receipts and cross checked that with the master military manifest and table of organizational equipment and all balanced.

For three months no one checked in or checked out a vehicle. Aaron literally had nothing to do while on duty and when he was off duty he spent most of his time in the base service club reading, watching TV, lifting weights in the workout room, or playing a pickup game of basketball or volleyball now and then. He did enroll in a graduate degree program through the base educational department and took a few courses in advanced cost accounting but found it not to his liking. He took another course in restaurant management thinking it might help him pick up some ideas on how to better run the family pizza business, but he was not exposed to any ideas or procedures that he had not already learned during his summer employments making pizzas.

He was very excited when one afternoon a young airman came in and said he needed to check out an additional staff car for the base commander. Aaron wondered why the base commander needed an additional staff car; the paper work the airman presented Aaron showed the base commander all ready had two, one for his wife and one for himself. As Aaron was perusing the paper work he took a little longer than the young airman thought necessary. "Look buddy," the airman snapped, "I haven't got all day, the Colonel wants the vehicle ten minutes ago, so hurry up and give me the keys."

"Let me see your ID again and I didn't know I was your buddy."

"OK, look Mac."

"Now that is better, Mac will do since my name is McShane, Aaron McShane and according to the paperwork you provided you are Wilson, Brian Wilson. How was the beach this summer?"

"Ya, that's right. Wilson, Brian Wilson. No relation in case you were going to ask, everyone else does."

"Ok Brian, come clean. What is going on? You wouldn't want to use the staff car for your own personal use, would you? Did you think you could just come in here and bluff your way to a sedan? Come on, Brian, give me a little credit. None of these signatures match. You got a hot date or something and want to impress her with something other than a two-ton truck?"

Brian hung his head and said, "That is about right."

"Well in that case, why didn't you just ask? I can always take care of a boy from Wyoming."

"How did you know I am from Wyoming?" was his bewildered response.

"It says so right here on your paperwork under home of record. Sure you can have a car. Just fill out the right forms. I don't even want to know how you got the base commander's signature. Oh God, you are dating his daughter aren't you? Well, I'll help fill out the forms in that case. I seem to be at the pinnacle of a mediocre career anyway. Oh by the way, I hear she has a young aunt visiting for the winter months. About my age isn't she?"

The weekends became much more fun than they had been. Wednesday night wasn't bad either - that is, when the base commander had his lodge meeting.

Brian and Aaron, along with the base commander's 18 year old daughter, Iris, and her 22 year old aunt, Melissa, sister of the colonel's young wife, explored Panama - or at least the western part - up and down the coast for a couple of miles north and south. The colonel was a nice enough guy from what Aaron's new friends said, but they also knew he would not have thought it proper for his daughter or sister-in-law to be dating men under his command, especially enlisted men, so they had to be careful.

The colonel's wife knew what was going on. She even helped the foursome by informing them of the commander's schedule so they would not show up at the same place. The four usually went to a little Panamanian bar just south of Panama City. The place had a porch open to the Pacific and many evenings were spent watching the sun set and ships sail out of sight.

Aaron and Brian had been in Panama for about six months and neither of them had ventured further than the little bar they were sitting in when the conversation started.

"Why don't we take a weekend trip some place instead of sitting around here all the time," asked Iris with a put-on pout.

"Why don't you ask your dad if you can get free tickets to watch Aaron and I be shot by a firing squad," Brian replied.

"Well I know something none of you know," said Melissa. "Sister and Ducky are attending a four week seminar in Washington, D.C. next month and leaving me as a chaperone to make sure that Iris doesn't do anything I wouldn't."

"That could be an interesting month for you, Brian," and Melissa swatted Aaron with a towel.

Ten minutes after the base commander and entourage left Panama for their trip to Washington the "fearless foursome" as they began calling themselves checked out a Land Rover from the motor pool, making sure the paperwork was in order, which made little difference because on his way out of the compound Aaron hung an official-looking sign on the gate stating the motor pool was closed until further notice. The authorizing signature was that of "Aaron McShane, Senior Motor Pool Operative." Everyone thought it looked official enough.

Melissa planned the excursion. First they would

drive across the Isthmus highway, which was really nothing more than a two lane road to Colon, where they would watch the ships line up to enter the canal. Then they would head down the coast and spend the night at an historic town called Portabella.

"There is a magnificent fort there. Just a few miles south of town is the famous Black Jesus shrine and further yet is the ancient and mysterious village called Nombre de Dios. It rests along the edge of a lagoon supporting a black sand beach. We will spend the night there and return the next morning to Camp Sheridan and then back here. The whole trip should not take more than a few days, and that is if we stop along the way and enjoy the sand and surf, which I most certainly plan on doing."

In reaching Colon they were all amazed at how many ships were lined up off the coast waiting their turn to enter the Canal. The mechanical mules and locks marveled them.

Aaron became angry with himself for spending the last few months not exploring the area. He was seeing things he had never seen before - not tremendous things but little things like a boy carrying over his shoulder a dead iguana, which would apparently be the family supper that night. On his way to Portabella he saw a man, woman and two children watching them as they drove past. The little family was sitting at a makeshift wooden table at the entrance of a hole dug into the side of a hill. It must have been their home, he thought to himself.

He saw little houses surrounded by banana trees. He had no idea that the banana fruit seemed to grow up side down. He stopped and talked to a man sitting on the ground surrounded by coconuts preparing them for sale at a market.

They stopped and got a small room in Portabella and before dinner they walked the remains of the fort where the Spanish had protected the route to Peru from those wanting to cash in on the gold and silver trade and where the Caribbean Spanish fleet was quartered to transport and protect the shipments of gold and silver to Spain.

The next day they took a leisurely drive further down the coast stopping whenever the littlest things seemed like they might be of interest, and they were. The flowering plants, the decorative vines and the abandoned cottages made their imaginations work overtime.

One site that would long be remembered by the Fearless Foursome was that of a cemetery where giant vultures perched on the tombstones. They stopped to gaze at such a macabre sight. It was Brian who started laughing. When the others questioned his sanity he told them to turn around and look. There behind them was a small slaughter house across the road from the cemetery. The vultures were just waiting for the leftovers from the next shipment of animals to be killed. "I suspect it is easier to let the vultures clean up the place than do it themselves," Iris quipped.

They were delayed in their journey only once,

through no fault or decision of their own, by cattle being herded down the middle of the road. The men doing the herding looked like actual cowboys minus the six-shooter. The herd eventually arrived at a pasture and Melissa said she now new what it meant to ride trail on a cattle drive in the old west.

They eventually came across an outdoor pool parlor and bar. They all ordered a beer and Brian and Aaron tried to shoot a game of pool. There were insects on the table along with leaves which made the game more challenging.

The outdoor pool hall was just on the outskirts of Nombre de Dios. They parked their vehicle alongside a vacant building and walked to the lagoon edging the village. Black sand squeezed between their toes as they walked barefoot around the lagoon.

Melissa: "This used to be the terminal for the gold and silver trade in the New World before the precious metals were forwarded to Spain, but the area around here used to be much more swampy than it is today and disease took its toll on man and beast. The operation was moved to Portabella. Unless you are a history buff you would only have heard about Nombre in a book called Portabella Gold. It was written as a prequel to Treasure Island twenty or so years after the death of Stevenson. A fan of his thought it would be nice to figure out where and how the treasure that Long John Silver sought was acquired and buried the first time. The book was not a best seller."

Aaron: "How do you know all this stuff?"

Melissa: "I didn't spend all my time crunching numbers; I've got a degree in history."

The Fearless Foursome spent the day exploring the Nombre and the surrounding area. They ate on a little porch that was not an actual restaurant but the owner of the hut indicated through broken English that she would cook them a meal for three dollars apiece. It wasn't bad. The fish was none that any of them had ever tasted or recognized by its appearance and the rice had an interesting blend of fruit and coconut.

They slept on the beach that night and the next morning decided to skip Fort Sheridan and headed back home. Aaron with all his bravado was getting a little anxious about the sign he hung on the motor pool gate and thought it ought to be removed sooner than later.

When they arrived back at Davis AFB, to their horror the base commander was waiting for them. The conference in Washington had been canceled and someone in the Pentagon failed to notify anyone in the Panama Canal Zone.

Because the base commander was a colonel and wanted to be a general, he did not want a scandal of any kind to blemish his record. He quietly put his sister-in-law on a plane to her home in Denver and he sent his daughter to an all-girl school in New Hampshire, while Brian was sent to Whiteman AFB in the middle of Missouri. That left only

Aaron. The colonel let Aaron stew for a while then cut orders for him to be sent to an administrative facility connected to a missile base in northwest Idaho where he was discharged one year later and went to work for the family pizza company.

CHAPTER 12
The Last Warrior

On the day Aaron McShane was discharged from the Air Force, Baylor McShane graduated from college with a teaching degree in elementary physical education and a commission as an Infantry Officer in the United State Army. He could not help himself (being what he considered a reluctant warrior) from being proud of both.

On the day he graduated he also received orders to report to Fort Benning, Georgia on January 10 the following year for the Infantry Officer Basic Course. He moved back home and took a job as a full time substitute teacher at his old high school.

Naturally, he met a girl. Naturally, he fell in love, And naturally, he got married even though the reporting date of January 10 was getting closer and closer. He sought a deferment to go to graduate school and was granted a one year induction extension.

One year after receiving his induction extension, he received another letter from the Army telling him that he would be sent orders to report to the

Infantry Officer Basic Course at a time that "is as yet to be determined." It advised him to do what was necessary to get his civilian affairs in order.

By this time he had become a father but there was no way of postponing the inevitable. In the same letter he was instructed to report to the contract physician named on the attachment for his pre-induction physical. The physician just happened to be the father of one of his students. After the examination the doctor took Baylor to his office and told Baylor that he was a borderline diabetic and that he could write the report any way Baylor wanted.

Baylor sat there in the doctor's office and realized this was his ticket out of having to go to Viet Nam. He had a wife, a child they called Junior and a job; who could blame him for not going especially if he flunked his physical. No one would know; he wouldn't even tell his wife.

The last few years had matured Baylor. He had taken his schooling seriously, approached his teaching position professionally, and accepted his responsibility of being a husband and parent with glee.

Half of his ROTC graduating class was serving on active duty and half of them were in Viet Nam. He knew at least two of them had a wife and child. Baylor made the only decision that an honorable person could make. He said he could not avoid going into the Army given the overall circumstance. He thanked the doctor for the offer.

Having successfully passed his physical and making arrangements to rent an apartment near Fort Benning for his little family who was going to get larger in six months, Baylor received a registered letter from the Department of Defense. The letter said that due to the current number of Infantry Officers awaiting active duty the Army had more supply than demand. "You still have an obligation to serve your country as a member of the armed forces, the letter stated, "but you may choose to apply for acceptance to an active or inactive National Guard or Reserve Unit." The letter went on to say that he still must report as ordered for the Infantry Officer Basic Course "unless you join an active or inactive Reserve or National Guard unit which at that point you will fall under their jurisdiction and follow their instructions accordingly."

There was a National Guard unit in Baylor's home town. He went and talked to the full time staff about the letter he received. He was told that there were several slots available but they were for qualified artillery officers. "I guess that lets me out I am in the Infantry," Baylor said.

"Well, unless you are in love with being in the infantry we can just transfer you to the artillery and send you to the Artillery Officers Basic Course at Fort Sill, Oklahoma. Trouble is, the next opening won't be until June 1 of the upcoming year. Does that present a problem?" the site commander asked.

Baylor McShane spent over twenty years in the

National Guard. He saw his unit grow from a good ole' boys club to a well run organization that anyone would be proud to be a member of. Most of his friends who had gone into the ROTC program only served the two years they were required. Some had asked for a one year deferment after graduation and prior to their reporting date received the same letter as he. Some chose the National Guard also and several of them served in the same Artillery Brigade and most of them ended up staying twenty years plus.

Baylor's military career was not as stellar as some of his peers but he managed to be efficient enough in the positions he had been assigned to always make the next promotion when he had to. Being a teacher, he had summer months off and took advantage of military schools and active duty opportunities as they arose. In addition, he participated in a division field training exercise in Germany and helped re-write the defense plan for Laverno, which required a trip to Pisa, Italy, near the American Army base called Camp Darby. He always wondered but never found out for sure if the camp was named after the Darby that had given him the ROTC test many years earlier.

There were two deployments of Baylor's that would have been of great personal significance and interest if any of the parties involved had known anything about their family history.

The Alaskan National Guard needed a training officer for a joint task force and requested applicants from National Guard units in the lower forty-eight. Alaska was conducting a school in unit and personal winter survival techniques at Fort Greely on Kodiak Island. Baylor applied and was accepted.

One evening over beer and poker, Baylor started talking to an Alaska Guardsman who it turned out had the same last name as his. Franklin McShane was an Engineering Officer acting as one of the primary cold weather instructors for the task force. He was an Alaskan Yupik Eskimo by law but not by culture. He was one quarter Yupik and had been born and raised in Anchorage. He had never been to his supposed ancestral village of Wilson Bay and wasn't inclined to do so, he told Baylor. He had a nice home, an Irish wife and parcel of little McShanes running about. He worked for an engineering consulting firm in Fairbanks when "not playing Army."

Neither man thought it was unduly strange that they both had the same last name. McShane was a common enough name and the two men laughed it off. "I can't wait until I get back home and tell my son he is related to a true to life Eskimo," said Baylor. From then till Baylor went home he and Franklin called each other "cousin", but only in jest.

The following year Baylor volunteered for a one month tour to help Panama's government build a coastal road between a village on the Atlantic side called Palinke to a little larger village north of there called Nombre de Dios. Nombre had easier access to the markets in Portabella.

As senior member of the advanced party, Baylor was obligated to meet with the local officials of both towns to insure peace and harmony would reign between the villagers and the soldiers. The Chief of Nombre was a tall fair-skinned Panamanian named Kona Scotty Niambi; the villagers just called him King. Baylor and Kona got along very well and shared many a meal on an open air porch overlooking the black sand lagoon. Neither ever suspected that they were somehow related.

On Baylor's flight back from Panama his group was informed that America had bombed Baghdad. It was the beginning of Desert Storm. Many guard units were called up from all 50 states. No one knew if and when their unit would be called.

Baylor was serving as the Intelligence Officer of a military unit. If activated, he would be responsible for "managing the turf," as it was said, in the rear area of a war zone. The organization was commanded by a colonel and in command of two Military Police Battalions, a Transportation Company and an Engineering Battalion. Any of those units could operate independently if necessary or be detached and attached to any other command element.

At a weekend field training exercise Baylor was notified that one of the subordinate units was to be activated. "We have one problem, Major McShane," said Colonel Myers,   "Major Simpson in the unit scheduled to be activated is not as of yet militarily qualified for the position he holds. He still has a few more courses to take and we do not think he will get them done in time. There are only two people in our command structure that are currently MOS qualified. Major Simpson's replacement will be either you or Major Danner. We don't make these types of decisions lightly or arbitrarily. I want to know what you think."

"Sir," said Baylor, "I have been putting on the pads for twenty years and if it comes time for me to get in the game how can I say I don't want to play." Baylor hated using the football metaphor as soon as it came out of his mouth but it was the only thing he could think to say at the time. He followed his comment by saying, "Let the system work, there is no reason I can think of as to why I should not go."

Two weeks had gone by when Baylor received a call from Colonel Myers, who told him that Major Simpson somehow managed to finish his correspondence courses sooner than anyone expected and would be qualified as far as the Army was concerned in a matter of just a few days and would accompany his unit to its activation station.

During and after Desert Storm there were several guard units from Baylor's state which were called up and continued to be called up but none affected Baylor directly. He retired from the guard six months later after failing his annual physical. He was diagnosed with type 2 diabetes and was declared by the Army as "not fit for service."

*****

The McShanes served the United States and its military in many ways, sometimes very reluctantly, but served nonetheless. There are undoubtedly many families that can say such a thing. The McShanes are one of many.

The Historical Section of the Pentagon, Military Archives, the Bureau of Census, personal diaries, letters and oral family history helped me chronicle the events herein described. According to the Department of Defense, there are no McShanes now serving in the Armed Forces of the United States. I suspect that won't last very long, however.

– Amos Hugh McShane
Proprietor
Lydia's Landing Inn

About the Author

Photo by Brian McAnally

Conley Stone "Snapper" McAnally is a retired U.S. Army Reserve officer and public school teacher. He is a former columnist for *The Examiner* of Independence, Missouri, where he cataloged his experience as a teacher in "bush" Alaska among the Yupik and Inupaque Eskimos. Several of his observations have been published in *Whispering Wind*, a magazine about Native American life and culture. His blog, The Adventures of Conley McAnally, is at conleymcanally.blogspot.com. He is also the the author of several short stories and novellas. He is the father of five children and grandfather of 15. He currently resides with his wife Beverly in Tucson, Arizona.

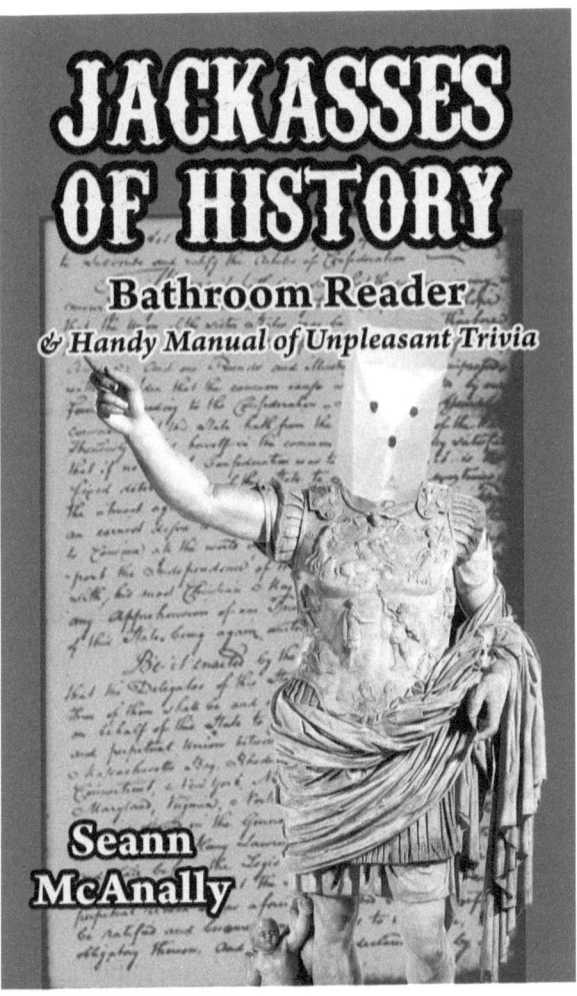

Pharaoh Publishing USA is an indepdendent publisher
of books, music and games in the Heart of America.

We do not accept unsolicited materials.

Contact us at pharaohpublishingusa@gmail.com.